Hurty Feelings

Helen Lester
Illustrated by Lynn Munsinger

Houghton Mifflin Harcourt
Boston   New York

For more information on the importance of feeling good about yourself and to download a free version of this story, visit

www.hmhbooks.com/freedownloads

Access code: confidence

Library of Congress Catalog Control Number 84-19212

HC ISBN 978-0-618-84062-5
POB ISBN 978-0-544-10622-2
Manufactured in China
SCP 10 9 8 7 6 5 4 3 2 1
4500440179

Fragility was a solid piece of work.

When she walked, her world wobbled.

In the hippo game "Sink to the Bottom" she was always the first to touch mud.

Her strong jaws could munch a field of grass faster than any lawn mower.

And she never cried when she stubbed one of her toes.

Or all sixteen.

But if injured toes didn't bother Fragility, something else did.
Injured feelings.
Fragility was fragile.

When someone said, "Fragility, you look so nice today," she would wail, "You hurt my *feeeee*lings!

Nice? Do you know what else is nice? Cupcakes are nice. So you're comparing me to a squishy cupcake."
With that she would flop on the ground and weep.

Or if someone said, "Fragility, you have such wonderful sturdy legs," she would wail, "You hurt my *feeeee*lings!
Sturdy legs? Do you know what else has sturdy legs? A piano has sturdy legs.

So you think I have piano legs."
And flop she'd go, weeping.

And if someone said, "Fragility, you have such cute little ears," she would wail, "You hurt my *feeeee*lings!
Cute little ears? Do you know what else has cute little ears?
People have cute little ears.

So you think I resemble a people?"
Flop. Weep.

As time went by, the other hippos, fearing she would throw
more fits, stopped speaking to Fragility, and she became
a big solid piece of —

loneliness.

One afternoon all of the hippos decided to play a game of pickup soccer.

Fragility had chomped the field to perfection. She stood solidly in the goal,

making save,

after save,

after save.

All was going well until . . .

RUDY appeared.
And Rudy had an appropriate name, for Rudy was extremely rude.
"I'm going to eat your goal," he announced, "for me lunch."
The hippos gasped in horror.

"Step aside, Big Solid Thing!" Rudy bellowed at Fragility. "You're blocking me lunch. I'm hungry and I don't have all day."

Fragility was frightened, but she was a solid piece of work, the Protector of the Goal, and thus she stood her ground. So Rudy, who knew of Fragility's fragile feelings, decided to dissolve her with insults. "You," said Rudy with a smirk, "are very gray and pudgy."

"Very gray and pudgy?" wailed Fragility. "Do you know what else is very gray and pudgy? An el . . ." The weeps took over, and she couldn't finish her sentence.

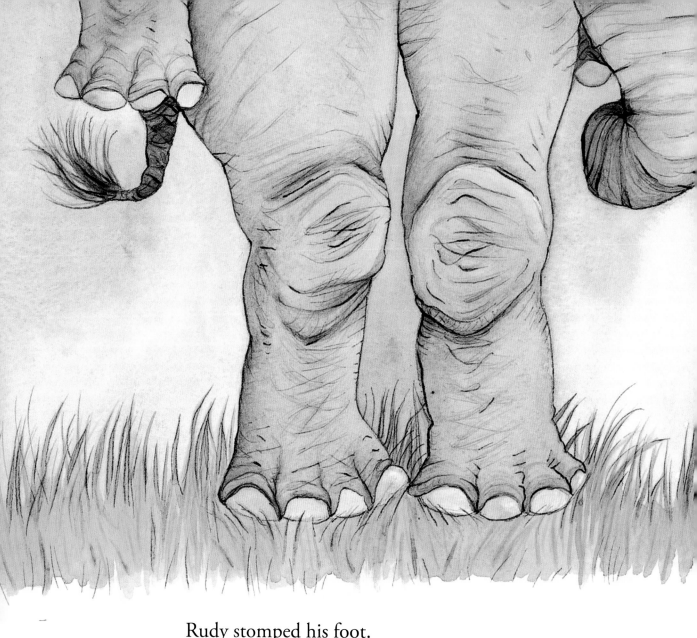

Rudy stomped his foot.
"There's no such thing as an el.
And stop weeping on me lunch.
By the way, you've got legs like tree stumps."

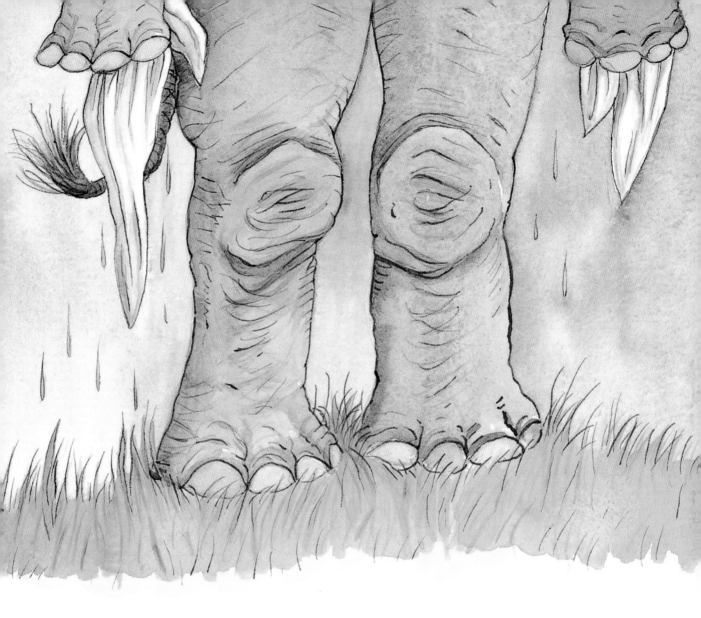

"Tree stumps?" wailed Fragility.
"Do you know what else has legs like tree stumps? An el . . .
eleph . . ."
The weeps took over, and she couldn't finish her sentence.

Rudy jumped up and down. "I've never heard of an el eleph. And I repeat, stop weeping on me lunch. You're making it soggy. Have you noticed your ears are just plain weird?"

"I'm weird-eared?" wailed Fragility. "Do you know what else has weird ears? An el . . . eleph . . . elephant!" Weeps and all, she finished her sentence.

"Elephant?" wondered Rudy.

"Seriously? Elephants have weird ears?"

He trotted over to the water tub and gazed at his reflection.

And his big, floppy, weird ears.

And his tree-stump legs.

And his very gray pudgy body.

Then he trotted back, flopped in front of the goal, and wailed,
"You hurt me *feeeee*lings!"

Seeing the big bully in such a state,
Fragility couldn't help but feel sorry for him.
She brought wet washcloths to soothe his red eyes,
and tissues so he could blow his trunk.

Then she cradled his head and cooed, "There, there.
I know just how you feel."

In time Rudy calmed down.
And he did not eat the hippos' goal.
He said he'd be back soon to cheer them in their game.
"But first I'm off for me lunch. A nice salad."

As he lumbered away, Rudy called, "Fragility, you're a solid piece of work."
"Solid piece of work?" she cried. "Do you know what else —"
And then she stopped short, smiled sweetly, and said,
"Why, thank you."